Dear Parents:

Congratulations! Your child is taking the first steps on an exciting journey. The destination? Independent reading!

STEP INTO READING® will help your child get there. The program offers five steps to reading success. Each step includes fun stories and colorful art or photographs. In addition to original fiction and books with favorite characters, there are Step into Reading Non-Fiction Readers, Phonics Readers and Boxed Sets, Sticker Readers, and Comic Readers—a complete literacy program with something to interest every child.

Learning to Read, Step by Step!

Ready to Read   Preschool–Kindergarten
• big type and easy words • rhyme and rhythm • picture clues
For children who know the alphabet and are eager to begin reading.

Reading with Help   Preschool–Grade 1
• basic vocabulary • short sentences • simple stories
For children who recognize familiar words and sound out new words with help.

Reading on Your Own   Grades 1–3
• engaging characters • easy-to-follow plots • popular topics
For children who are ready to read on their own.

Reading Paragraphs   Grades 2–3
• challenging vocabulary • short paragraphs • exciting stories
For newly independent readers who read simple sentences with confidence.

Ready for Chapters   Grades 2–4
• chapters • longer paragraphs • full-color art
For children who want to take the plunge into chapter books but still like colorful pictures.

STEP INTO READING® is designed to give every child a successful reading experience. The grade levels are only guides; children will progress through the steps at their own speed, developing confidence in their reading.

Remember, a lifetime love of reading starts with a single step!

Copyright © 2020 Disney Enterprises, Inc. All rights reserved. Published in the United States by Random House Children's Books, a division of Penguin Random House LLC, 1745 Broadway, New York, NY 10019, and in Canada by Penguin Random House Canada Limited, Toronto, in conjunction with Disney Enterprises, Inc.

Step into Reading, Random House, and the Random House colophon are registered trademarks of Penguin Random House LLC.

Visit us on the Web!
StepIntoReading.com
rhcbooks.com

Educators and librarians, for a variety of teaching tools, visit us at RHTeachersLibrarians.com

ISBN 978-0-7364-4053-0 (trade) — ISBN 978-0-7364-8290-5 (lib. bdg.)
ISBN 978-0-7364-4054-7 (ebook)

Printed in the United States of America   10 9 8 7 6 5 4 3 2

𝒟ɪsɴᴇʏ

MULAN

by Mary Tillworth

illustrated by the Disney Storybook Art Team

Random House 🏠 New York

Mulan is a young woman.

She lives in

a small village.

She is smart and strong.

One day,

men on horses bring news.

There is a war!

One man from each family

must join the army.

Mulan's father is the only
man in Mulan's family.
He has orders
to join.

Mulan knows her father
is too old to go to war.
She will take his place.
She cuts off her hair.

She puts on armor.
Now she looks like a man.
She rides off to join
the army.

Shang is the army trainer.
Mulan gives him
her father's army orders.

Her plan works!

Shang thinks she is a man.

Shang tells the men
to climb a tall pole.

They all fail.

Mulan does not give up.

She makes it to the top!

Shang leads Mulan
and the men into battle.
They fight Shan-Yu
and his army.

Shang's army is brave.
But Shan-Yu's army
is very big.

Mulan meets a spirit dragon
named Mushu.
She uses him
to light a cannon.
She stops Shan-Yu!

Mulan is hurt.

A doctor treats her.

Then he tells Shang

that Mulan is a woman.

Shang is angry.

Mulan learns Shan-Yu
is coming after them!
She tries to warn Shang.
He does not listen.

Shan-Yu captures Shang!

Mulan will save him.

She holds her hair back.

Now Shan-Yu sees the soldier

who defeated his army!

Mulan and Shan-Yu fight.

Mulan pins Shan-Yu

to the roof.

Mushu soars in with a rocket.

The rocket stops
Shan-Yu.

Mulan and Shang
watch fireworks from
the rocket light the sky.

The emperor thanks Mulan.
He bows to honor her.
Shang and the other soldiers
bow to her, too.

Mulan returns to her village.

She hugs her father.

He is very proud of his

brave Mulan.